Hi, I'm Philip. I've been on work experience at Premier supermarket for two weeks. No kidding!
I worked from 9am to 4pm every day.
I'll tell you how I got on.

1

On my first day, I woke up early.

I was feeling a bit sick.

Dad said it was just nerves. I put on my uniform and Dad did my tie.

Then Elaine arrived to take me to work.

Elaine helps me at school. She's nice.

"Hey! Who's this smart young man? Do I know you?" she said.

She likes to pull my leg.

Dad wished me good luck.

Then we set off.

First day induction
Identity badges
Keeping alert and safe

At the supermarket, we met Donna,

my supervisor.

She took us round the store and showed

us where everything was.

She gave us identity badges to wear.

I was just fixing my badge when a

man nearly ran his trolley into me.

Elaine called out, "Wake up, Philip!"

Donna was smiling.

Premier
Philip Ali
Trainee

Premier
Donna Jones
Supervisor

Premier
Elaine Evans
Visitor

Donna showed me how to find things in the store.

"These signs tell you where things are," she said.

"And all the aisles have numbers."

Then Donna took us to the back of
the store.

"Customers aren't allowed through here,"
she said.

You had to tap in a number to open
the door.

I was worried that I would forget it.

"Write it down, then," said Elaine.

We went to the staffroom.

"You come here for your breaks,"
said Donna.

She showed us the toilets, and I was
given a locker for my things.

"You get a 15-minute break at 10.45,
and another break at 3 o'clock in
the afternoon.

Your lunch break will be from 12.15
to 1.15pm."

There was a big notice on the wall.

"These are our golden rules," said Donna.

"You must remember them."

Elaine helped me for the first week.

One morning we stacked shelves

with biscuits.

We had to look at the sell-by dates.

The new biscuits had to go at the back.

But I got into a bit of a muddle.

OK, so I'm a bit thick.

"Let's take it slowly," said Elaine.

"You'll get the hang of it."

Elaine wasn't with me for the
second week.

I worked with the customers.

Most customers were nice but one man
was really nasty.

He asked me where the eggs were.

I looked at the signs but I couldn't see
the word 'eggs'.

"You're not much use, are you?" he said.

"I'll find them myself!"

"I'm sorry," I said, "I'm new here."

I found Donna. I asked her to help
the man.

I told her what had happened.

"You handled that well," she said.

"The eggs are next to the bread."

One day I had to pack at the check-out.
Donna showed me what to do.
I put heavy things at the bottom of
the bags.
I put light things on the top.
One woman was in a hurry. She left a
jar of coffee behind.
I ran after her with it. The woman said
I was a star!

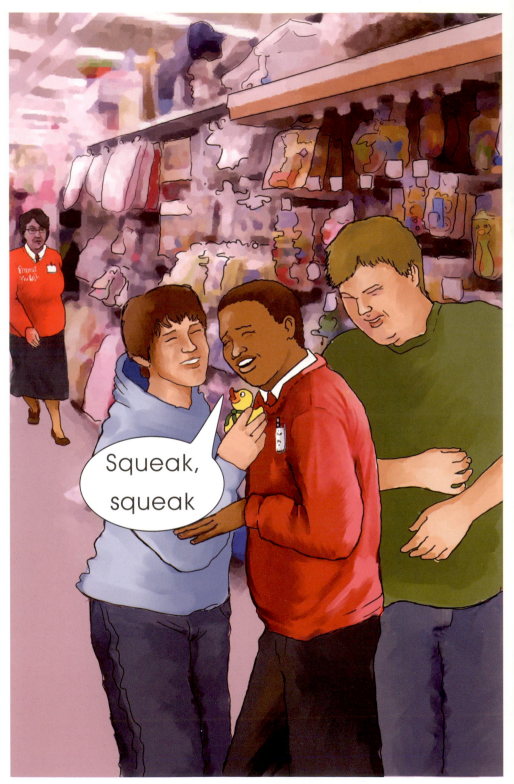

But Thursday was a bad day.

My mates came into the store.

We all started messing about.

Donna saw us and she was a bit cross.

"You're not here to chat, Philip," she said.

"You're here to work!"

I felt bad. I had let myself down.

Friday was my last day. It was a crazy day. So much happened!
Donna said I was a good worker.
I felt proud of myself.

I learned a lot at
the supermarket and
I think I did all right.
One day I'd like to
work there for real.

How well did Philip do?

24